CW00499014

Noughts & Crosses

Contents

OXFORD
UNIVERSITY PRESS

Great Clarendon Street, Oxford OX2 6DP

Oxford University Press is a department of the University of Oxford. It furthers the University's objective of excellence in research, scholarship, and education by publishing worldwide in

Oxford New York

Auckland Cape Town Dar es Salaam Hong Kong Karachi Kuala Lumpur Madrid Melbourne Mexico City Nairobi New Delhi Shanghai Taipei Toronto

With offices in

Argentina Austria Brazil Chile Czech Republic France Greece Gautemala Hungary Italy Japan South Korea Poland Portugal Singapore Switzerland Thailand Turkey Ukraine Vietnam

Oxford is a registered trade mark of Oxford University Press in the UK and in certain other countries

Text © Frances Gregory 2008

The moral rights of the author have been asserted

Database right Oxford University Press (maker)

First published 2008

All rights reserved. No part of this publication may be reproduced, stored in a retrieval system, or transmitted in any form or by any means, without the prior permission in writing of Oxford University Press, or as expressly permitted by law, or under terms agreed with the appropriate reprographics rights organization. Enquiries concerning reproduction outside the scope of the above should be sent to the Rights Department, Oxford University Press, at the address above.

You must not circulate this book in any other binding or cover and you must impose this same condition on any acquirer.

British Library Cataloguing in Publication Data

Data available

ISBN 978 019 832855 1

10 9 8 7 6 5 4 3 2 1

Printed in China by Printplus

Acknowledgements

The Publisher would like to thank the following for permission to reproduce photographs:

P3: RHCB; p6: Getty Images; p8: Bettmann/Corbis; p9l: Burt Shavitz/Pix Inc/Time Life Pictures/Getty Images: p9r: Wikimedia; p10: Rob & SAS/Corbis; p12: Bridgeman Art Library; p13: Moviestore; p15: Rex Features.

Illustrations are by Steve Evans

We are grateful for permission to reprint the following copyright material in this guide:

Malorie Blackman: extracts from *Noughts and Crosses* (Doubleday, 2001), reprinted by permission of the Random House Group Ltd. Letter to the Reader and extracts from author's website: www.malorieblackman.co.uk including quotations from the media, reprinted by permission of the author.

Paul Kelbie: extract from 'Racists are jailed for life after abducting and killing boy, 15', The Independent, 8.11.2006, copyright © The Independent 2006, reprinted by permision of Independent News and Media Ltd.

Stephen Sondheim: extract from lyrics to 'Somewhere' from *West Side Story*, copyright © 1956, 1957 Amberson Holdings LLC and Stephen Sondheim, reprinted by permission of Universal Music/ Music Sales

Alan Travis: extract from '"Race Murder" charges dropped', *The Guardian*, 30.7.1993, copyright © Guardian News and Meida 1993, reprinted by permission of Guardian News and Media Ltd.

Benjamin Zephaniah: 'White Comedy' from *Propa Propaganda* (Bloodaxe Books, 1996), reprinted by permission of the publisher.

WGBH: abridged synopsis for 'A Class Divided', copyright © 2005 WGBH/Boston, reprinted by permission of Frontline and WBGH Educational Foundation.

We have tried to trace and contact all copyright holders before publication. If notified, the publisher will be pleased to rectify any errors or omissions at the earliest opportunity.

A Letter from Malorie Blackman

Dear Reader

I'd been mulling over the idea of writing a story about slavery for quite a while, but the reaction from my friends was lukewarm to say the least. 'Slavery is in the past', 'Why d'you want to rehash something so painful?', 'Why do black people always harp on about slavery?' are just a few of the comments I received. Almost everyone I spoke to about it was of the view 'Been there, done that, let's move on'. But I wanted to write a story about the legacy of slavery. About how attitudes way back when, still influence all our lives and the way we think and live today.

I really believe the subject of slavery is terribly important – especially in this day and age. I think it gives a context to modern day western world thinking and attitudes regarding other races and cultures.

But the comments and feedback I received planted the seed of the idea for *Noughts and Crosses* in my mind. It occurred to me that the story I had in mind would be more challenging to write and hopefully read if I played with people's perceptions of the society presented in the story. I wanted to turn society as we know it on its head in my story, with new names for the major divisions in society, i.e. noughts (the underclass) and Crosses (the majority, ruling society). I wanted to see this new world through the eyes of the two main characters, Callum (a nought) and Sephy (a Cross). Race and racism are emotive issues that most people are loath to discuss but I think they should be discussed, no matter how painful.

Noughts and Crosses is a game that no one really plays much past childhood because once you've grasped its objective and tactics, it invariably ends in a draw – a no-win situation… I think that pretty much sums up racism. Ultimately no one wins. And as was said by Abraham Joshua Heschel, 'Racism is man's gravest threat to man – the maximum of hatred for a minimum of reason'.

Malorie Blackman

Whose Viewpoint?

Think, pair, share

- When someone tries to give you advice or tells you what to do, do you say, 'But you don't understand – you can't possibly – you're not me!'
- Do you find yourself changing your mind about something once you've seen someone else's point of view?
- When you read a book by someone or about someone very different from you, does it help you to see some things from another point of view? Can we ever really know what it's like to be in someone else's shoes?

An author's viewpoint

These facts can be found on Malorie Blackman's website:

She is one of the first generation of British-born black writers. In 2003 she was the only black writer in the top 100 of the BBC's *The Big Read*, listing the nation's favourite books.

As a child, she loved reading fantasies, mysteries and love stories, but remembers that they never featured a black child.

When she was at school the careers teacher told her that black girls didn't become English teachers.

One day, when she went to buy some plasters, she found herself questioning why they were always pink.

She has been called 'jungle bunny' by white boys outside her local supermarket, and black guys have called her a slag because she has a daughter who is of mixed race.

When she started writing for children, she discovered that some publishers expected her to write about race and nothing else.

Discuss: How might these facts have influenced Malorie Blackman's viewpoint and her choices when she came to write?

As you read *Noughts and Crosses*, notice how Malorie Blackman uses her own experiences in the story or in her presentation of characters.

Whose Viewpoint?

Narrative viewpoint

Why does Malorie Blackman have two different points of view in her novel? Apart from the opening chapter, half the story is told by Callum and the other half comes from Sephy. Both narrators speak in the first person.

Why did Malorie Blackman do that?

Below is her answer:

I wanted the society in my book to be viewed from two different points of view (Callum and Sephy's) to show how our perspectives colour our thinking. The adage, 'you can't really know someone until you have walked in their shoes', is like all clichés mostly true. That I think was the idea I had in mind when I sat down to write Noughts and Crosses.

As you read, make a note of the differences between Callum's and Sephy's perspectives on things:

- What different views do they have about each other's homes?
- How does each of them feel about the other's family?
- How does each feel about Callum's arrival at Heathcroft?
- Why is it hard for Sephy to understand Callum's anger when she uses the word 'blanker' to condemn her fellow students?

Think: What do *you* think the novel gains from having both viewpoints?

Ongoing task: Keep this question in mind as you read the novel.

It's Just a Word

White Comedy

By Benjamin Zephaniah

I waz whitemailed
By a white witch,
Wid white magic
An white lies,
Branded by a white sheep
I slaved as a whitesmith
Near a white spot
Where I suffered whitewater fever.
Whitelisted as a whiteleg
I waz in de white book
As a master of white art,
It waz like white death.

People called me a white jack
Some hailed me as a white wog,
So I joined de white watch
Trained as a white guard
Lived off the white economy.
Caught and beaten by de whiteshirts
I waz condemned to a white mass,
Don't worry,
I shall be writing to de Black House.

Think, pair, share

What point is the poet making?

Black and white

How do we use those two simple words? Here are some prompts from the dictionary (taken from the *Oxford School Dictionary*):

Black economy – employment where payments are concealed to avoid tax

Blackguard – a wicked person (originally the servants who did all the dirty jobs)

Blackleg – a person who works while fellow workers are on strike

Blacklist – to put someone on a list of those who are disapproved of

Blackmail – to demand money from someone by threatening to reveal a secret

Black market – illegal trading

Black sheep – a disgraced member of a family

Blackspot – a dangerous place

It's Just a Word

White lie – *a harmless lie to avoid hurting someone's feelings*

Whitewash – *concealing a mistake*

White elephant – *a useless possession*

There are many more negative connotations for the word 'black', aren't there? Think of all the positive associations for the word 'white'. Are there any negative associations of 'white'?

Task

Check for yourself in any dictionary and decide which word carries the greatest negativity.

Noughts and crosses

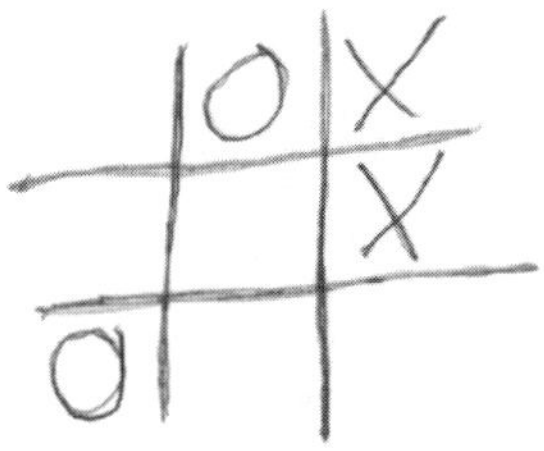

In a game of noughts and crosses, is one superior to the other? How does Malorie Blackman exploit the meaning of the word 'nought' to create her underclass in *Noughts and Crosses*? (Have you noticed that Crosses always get a capital C, while noughts are given a lower-case letter? Look out for a change towards the end of the novel.)

Look at these comments from Sephy and Callum:

'STOP IT! YOU'RE ALL BEHAVING LIKE ANIMALS!... WORSE THAN ANIMALS – LIKE BLANKERS!' Sephy (page 58)

'I'm not a blanker. I may be a nought but I'm worth more than nothing. I'm not a blanker. A waste of time and space. A zero... I'M NOT A BLANKER' Callum (page 59)

'Sticks and stones, Callum. It's one word, that's all.' Sephy (page 59)

Think, pair, share

Why does Sephy use this word? Why is this one word so offensive to Callum?

What words do you find most offensive? What words hurt you most?

Do the people who use these words know they are being offensive? Or are they, like Sephy, just using words they've heard others use?

Where in the World?

Where in the world do you think *Noughts and Crosses* is set? Where's your evidence in the novel?

> I drew on many different societies so bits of it were the Southern states of America, bits of it were South Africa, bits of it were Northern Ireland, when the troubles were going on, and so on. So in my head it's kind of set in an alternative Britain... [it] was inspired by things like the Stephen Lawrence case and things that happened to me in my own childhood.
>
> Malorie Blackman, quoted on the BBC's Blast website, www.bbc.co.uk/blast/writing/people/malorie_blackman.shtml

How might the historical events and characters described on these pages have inspired aspects of *Noughts and Crosses*?

Black American heroes

What similarities are there in the true story below to Callum's experience at Heathcroft School?

The Little Rock Nine

The Little Rock Nine is the name given to the first black teenagers to attend the all-white Central High School in Little Rock, Arkansas, in 1957.

Those who supported racist school systems defied the law which forbade segregation – by intimidating black students. On the first day of school, the state's National Guard were ordered to prevent the black students from entering the school. President Eisenhower had to send in federal troops to protect them.

The Little Rock Nine were determined to receive the same education as white students. Every morning on their way to school angry crowds of white people taunted and insulted them – they even received death threats. But though they were frightened, the students wouldn't give up. These nine teenagers challenged a racist system and defeated it.

What hopes does Callum have for his future at Heathcroft? Will he succeed in challenging the prejudice of his society as the Little Rock Nine did?

Where in the World?

Martin Luther King

Martin Luther King was a leader of the civil rights movement in America. He advocated non-violent resistance against unjust laws, believing that it ennobled the person who used it. He was shot dead in 1968.

Malcolm X

Another influential figure in the American civil rights movement was known as Malcolm X. He had a different view of the struggle for equality, believing it was right to fight racial injustice 'by any means necessary'. He was shot dead in 1965.

Are either of these philosophies represented in *Nought and Crosses*?

Malorie Blackman says: 'The resentment of Jude (Callum's brother) for the Crosses, stems from the fact that he was not allowed to stay on at school even though he wanted to and he's not allowed to play his full part in the society he lives in… but there are various ways of doing something about that. Jude, unfortunately, chooses violence… Callum's family do have a number of ordeals to live through, but some, if not all of these, are issues that ethnic minorities have to deal with on a regular basis in real life, i.e. inequalities in education, health, the justice system, employment and access to opportunity.'

Think, pair, share

Do you think violence is ever justified in opposing racial inequality?

Racism in England

'Race murder' charges dropped

Fears of renewed racial violence in south-east London were raised yesterday after charges against two teenagers accused of murdering a black schoolboy, Stephen Lawrence, were dropped. The Crown Prosecution Service said there was 'insufficient evidence to provide a realistic prospect of a conviction' in a case which has sparked anti-racist demonstrations across London.

Racists jailed for life

The murder of a white schoolboy by a gang of Asians almost tore apart a community that was already rife with racial tensions. As details emerged of how the 15-year-old boy was dragged from the street, taken on a terrifying 200-mile drive, beaten, stabbed and burnt to death there were fears that Glasgow could erupt into racial violence... Kriss was picked on purely because of the colour of his skin.

Research

Explore and discuss other recent conflicts that might have influenced Malorie Blackman's depiction of racial and social divisions in *Nought and Crosses*. Start by rereading and following up her comments at the top of page 8. What part did violence play in these conflicts, and were any of them resolved without violence?

Blue Eyes, Brown Eyes – A True Story

On the day after Martin Luther King was murdered in April 1968, Jane Elliott's third graders from the small, all-white town of Riceville, Iowa, came to class confused and upset. They recently had made King their 'Hero of the Month', and they couldn't understand why someone would kill him. So Elliott decided to teach her class a daring lesson in the meaning of discrimination…

Elliott divided her class by eye color – those with blue eyes and those with brown. On the first day, the blue-eyed children were told they were smarter, nicer, neater, and better than those with brown eyes. Throughout the day, Elliott praised them and allowed them privileges… In contrast, the brown-eyed children had to wear collars around their necks and their behavior and performance were criticized and ridiculed by Elliott. On the second day, the roles were reversed…

What happened over the course of the unique two-day exercise astonished both students and teacher. On both days, children who were designated as inferior took on the look and behavior of genuinely inferior students, performing poorly on tests and other work. In contrast, the 'superior' students – students who had been sweet and tolerant before the exercise – became mean-spirited and seemed to like discriminating against the 'inferior' group.

Think, pair, share

What does this suggest about any form of discrimination by colour?
You can read much more detail and watch video recordings of this fascinating and historic experiment at this web address: www.pbs.org/wgbh/pages/frontline/shows/divided/etc/view.html

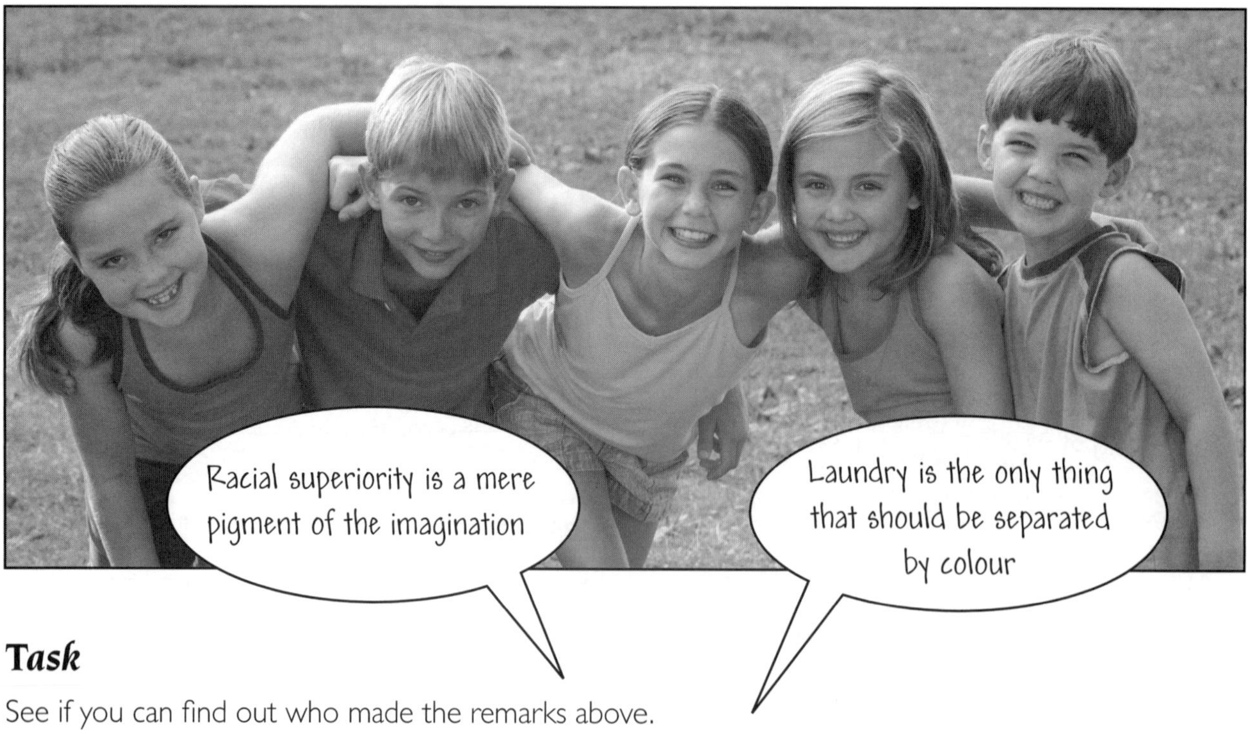

Task

See if you can find out who made the remarks above.
Can you find other memorable comments about colour discrimination?

Black Skin, White Skin – A Writer's Story

Malorie Blackman has said that racism is 'one of those things people have to be ever vigilant about otherwise things will get worse. I think part of the way of doing that is to have more culturally and ethnically diverse books and encourage children to read as widely as possible. If children learn about different cultures, different religions and different races, you won't get the ignorance that leads to fear.'

Before she wrote *Noughts and Crosses* (it was her fiftieth book) Malorie Blackman had not tackled racism head on: 'I wanted to read books that had me in them… I wanted a black person on the cover, but plots that had nothing to do with racism.'

Think, pair, share

Why did she wait until her fiftieth book before tackling racism? What further answers can you find in the text below?

'I wanted to play with assumptions, and I wanted people to be surprised when they read it, just to make people talk about things... A lot of it was based on things that happened to me, like the teacher and school experiences... there are so many more I could have put in there... of all the characters I've written, I think that Callum's experiences are the closest to mine... I find that really funny, really ironic... a white boy. That's why it was a difficult book to write, shifting things 180 degrees. That's why I don't think I was ready to write it ten years ago, even five years ago. I needed to do all these other things. If I had written it ten years ago, five years ago even, I would have been constantly censoring myself.'

Read more of Malorie Blackman's views at this web address:
www.bbc.co.uk/blast/writing/people/malorie_blackman.shtml

Star-Crossed Lovers

> *A number of people have stated that* Noughts and Crosses *is based on* Romeo and Juliet. *It may well be, but I promise that when I sat down to write the story, that's not what I was thinking... As I wrote the story however, I became aware of the parallels.*
>
> *Malorie Blackman*

What do you think?

Romeo and Juliet

Set in Verona, the story centres round a feud between the families of the Montagues and the Capulets. Romeo and Juliet belong to opposing sides of this violent feud.

Romeo and Juliet fall instantly in love after meeting at a party. After the party, Romeo daringly climbs up to Juliet's balcony and the couple declare their love. Secretly, they marry. No sooner are they united than Romeo is involved in a fatal fight with Juliet's violent cousin, Tybalt, whom he kills. For this, Romeo is banished from Verona.

As her parents are ignorant of her marriage to Romeo, she is forced to agree to another marriage. To delay this, she takes a potion that will make everyone think she is dead, but in fact she will revive. A letter is sent to Romeo to warn him to ignore reports of Juliet's death, but an outbreak of the plague prevents the letter from reaching him. Hearing of her death, he returns to Verona, carrying with him some truly lethal poison. He arrives at her tomb just before she recovers consciousness. Believing she is dead, he poisons himself and dies. Seconds later she awakes and, finding him dead beside her, takes her own life.

Romeo and Juliet's deaths reconcile the two families and the feud ends.

Think, pair, share

What are the differences and similarities between the two stories?

Star-Crossed Lovers

The old, old story

The Romeo and Juliet plot forms the basis of many other stories, including musicals and films. *West Side Story*, for example, resets the tragic tale in America. Sephy and Callum's words in *Noughts and Crosses* 'another place… another time' (page 383) echo the words of a song from the musical:

There's a place for us
Somewhere a place for us
Peace and quiet and open air
Wait for us
Somewhere

There's a time for us
Some day a time for us
Time together with time to spare
Time to learn, time to care
Some day
Somewhere…

The shape of tragedy

One important defining feature of tragedy is the bad choices made by the leading characters. Malorie Blackman admits:

When I get an idea for a story, I tend to get the general plot in my head first, but for me, the characters make or break a story. I have to care about them to care about the plot so I spend more time on trying to get the characters right before I start writing than on anything else. I don't necessarily have to sympathise with everything the main characters do but I feel I should empathise with them, that is I should understand what motivates and drives them – even if I disagree with their ultimate actions. Callum is a case in point. I grew really attached to his character but I think he makes some terrible choices. But then, so does Sephy!

Check

What bad choices has each of them already made?
In tragedy, bad choices have fatal consequences. The characters almost seemed doomed from the start. What clues run through *Noughts and Crosses* that the story will end unhappily?

Task

Collect hints that things will end unhappily as you read on.

Readers Writing About *Noughts And Crosses*

BOOKS Galore

Book Reviews

HOME

BOOKS

AUTHORS

REVIEWS

'It got me thinking and I started comparing it to things happening in the news. I found the end pretty depressing though, and I don't think everyone would enjoy that.'

'It's an up-to-date story where Callum, a nought (a second-class citizen) tries to stay friends with Sephy, a Cross (his social superior). No one can accept their friendship, their families are torn apart and Callum gets involved in terrorism. It is similar to *Romeo and Juliet* except it's better.'

'The main characters are Sephy and Callum and the narrative constantly switches between their different points of view. It is easy to sympathize with these characters, but there were times when I hated how they treated each other.'

'The themes are excellent: romance, politics and terrorism. Although it's obviously a love story, it's also dark and political. I particularly like the way the language of the two first-person narratives reflects how the two characters mature as time passes.'

'The noughts don't have a Nelson Mandela or a Martin Luther King – they just have their terrorist Liberation Militia. It's as if they are motivated by mere hatred, not the desire for equality.'

'Blackman's decision to subvert our expectations of race by making the ruling classes black and the oppressed group white is masterly. This simple choice proves highly effective in raising the reader's awareness of the arbitrary nature of colour discrimination. When Callum has to use a black plaster on his white skin, you realize, with a shock, that this is the sort of invisible discrimination our society condones. Malorie Blackman also makes us question how history has been told – has one racial group airbrushed out the achievements of another to maintain power?'

Readers Writing About *Noughts And Crosses*

Your views?

- How far do you agree with these other readers?
- What other points would you like to suggest?
- Share your views with a partner and your class.

Audience and purpose

Your next task is to persuade a teacher who has not read *Noughts and Crosses* of the value of the novel to a year 9 class. If you wish, you could choose to convince your head teacher to buy a set of books for next year.

Questions to consider

- How will you present your case? What visual aids will you use?
- How much of the plot will you reveal?
- What will you say about the characters and relationships?
- What will you say about the novel's themes and the issues that it raises, and how these relate to your life and experience?
- Will you read out sections of the text? Which parts might you choose?
- What secondary sources might add colour and detail to your presentation? You might use Malorie Blackman's website, www.malorieblackman.co.uk, or book club websites.
- Might you use some of the information you have found in this *Reading Guide*?

Other important things to remember

- Use formal language suited to your audience
- Select specific evidence from the text or from other sources to back up your case
- Use persuasive language that will convince the listener.

Writing up your findings

Present your case in writing, outlining your resources, to your teacher so that he or she can select the most persuasive presentations to be delivered to an invited audience.

Pathways... to Another Good Read

Works by the same author

Knife Edge
ISBN 978-055-254892-2
The second volume of the trilogy: this one tracks the fortunes of Jude McGregor.

Checkmate
ISBN 978-055-255194-6
The final part of the trilogy follows Callie Rose.

Hacker
ISBN 978-055-255164-9
Vicky hacks into the bank's computer files to prove her dad is innocent of crimes for which he lost his job.

A.N.T.I.D.O.T.E.
ISBN 978-055-255168-7
Elliot discovers that his mum is a spy and she's in serious trouble.

Unheard Voices
ISBN 978-055-255600-2
Malorie Blackman's anthology of stories and poems about slavery.

Novels about discrimination and social division

Divided City by Theresa Breslin
ISBN 978-019-832674-8
Divisions between Catholics and Protestants, Rangers and Celtic supporters are the backdrop for the arrival of an asylum seeker.

The Innocent's Story by Nicky Singer
ISBN 978-019-272617-9
A terrorist plants a bomb in the city centre and there are unpredictable consequences.

Across The Barricades by Joan Lingard
ISBN 978-014-037179-6
In this story of star-crossed lovers, the opposition between Protestants and Catholics during the troubles in Northern Ireland is the focus.

The Outsiders by S.E. Hinton
ISBN 978-014-131457-0
This is a classic tale of gang rivalry in urban America.

Roll of Thunder, Hear My Cry by Mildred Taylor
ISBN 978-014-037174-1
Set in post-slavery southern states of America, this novel charts the fortunes and misfortunes of a share-cropping black family and their neighbours.

The Whisper by Bali Rai
ISBN 978-055-254891-5
A sequel to *The Crew*, this novel explores real-life issues for teenagers in multicultural Britain.

Nightjohn by Gary Paulsen
ISBN 978-033-033604-8
This book follows the fortunes of a 12-year-old black American slave girl.

Small Island by Andrea Levy
ISBN 978-075-530749-4
Levy offers insights into the life of Afro-Caribbean immigrants to Britain after the Second World War.